Will   Irma   Taranee   Cornelia   Hay Lin

GRAPHIC NOVEL #1

THE POWER OF FRIENDSHIP

W.i.t.c.h.

Will   Irma   Taranee   Cornelia   Hay Lin

GRAPHIC NOVEL #1

THE POWER OF FRIENDSHIP

an imprint of
HYPERION BOOKS FOR CHILDREN
New York

© 2005 Disney Enterprises, Inc.
W.I.T.C.H., Will Irma Taranee Cornelia Hay Lin is a trademark of Disney Enterprises, Inc.
Volo® is a registered trademark of Disney Enterprises, Inc.
Volo/Hyperion Books for Children are imprints of Disney Children's Book Group, L.L.C.

Printed in the United States of America

First Edition
1 3 5 7 9 10 8 6 4 2

ISBN 0-7868-3674-1

Visit www.clubwitch.com

DISTANT AND DEEP . . .

THIS IS CANDRACAR . . . AN ELSEWHERE WITH NEITHER TIME NOR SPACE.

A VAST NOTHINGNESS IN THE CENTER OF WHICH RISES UP THE TEMPLE OF THE CONGREGATION . . .

ALLOW ITS SPLENDOR TO DAZZLE YOUR EYES. COME CLOSER IF YOU DARE, BUT DO SO IN SILENCE. . . .

THE ORACLE IS ABOUT TO SPEAK. . . .

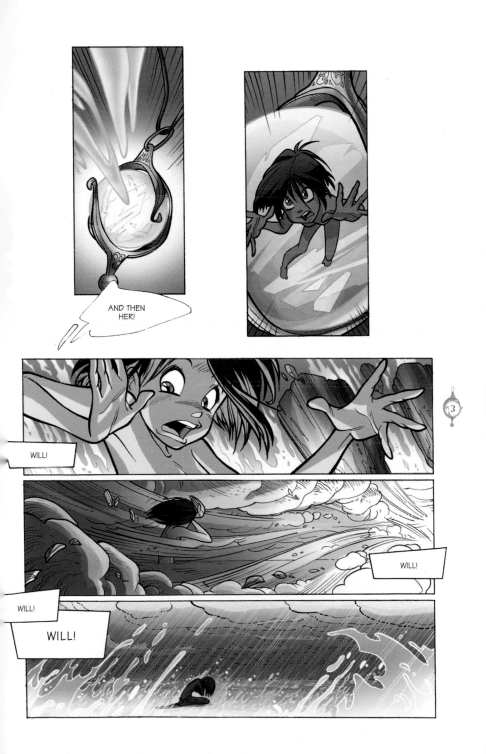

27

LET ME TELL YOU A STORY, GIRLS! A STORY AS OLD AS TIME . . .

". . . A DISTANT TIME WHEN EVERYTHING WAS YOUNG, AND SPIRITS AND CREATURES LIVED UNDER THE SAME SKY!

". . . UNTIL SPIRITS AND CREATURES LEARNED EVIL, AND THIS ONE WORLD WAS DIVIDED INTO TWO PARTS: ONE FOR THOSE WHO WANTED PEACE AND ONE FOR THOSE WHO LIVED ON OTHERS' PAIN.

E UNIVERSE A SINGLE, MMENSE INGDOM ULED BY ATURE— KINGDOM THAT LASTED ONS. . . .

"BEFORE SEPARATING FOR ETERNITY, THE UNIVERSE GAVE LIFE TO THE FORTRESS OF CANDRACAR, IN THE VERY HEART OF INFINITY.

47

"TO SEPARATE THE TWO HALVES, THE VEIL WAS CREATED. EVIL AND INJUSTICE WERE BANISHED TO THE DARK SIDE OF METAMOOR.

"THERE, THE MIGHTIEST SPIRITS AND CREATURES ARE ON GUARD . . ."

THERE, THE PROTECTORS OF THE VEIL RESIDE, AND THERE, IF YOU WISH, YOU ALSO MAY JOURNEY.

55

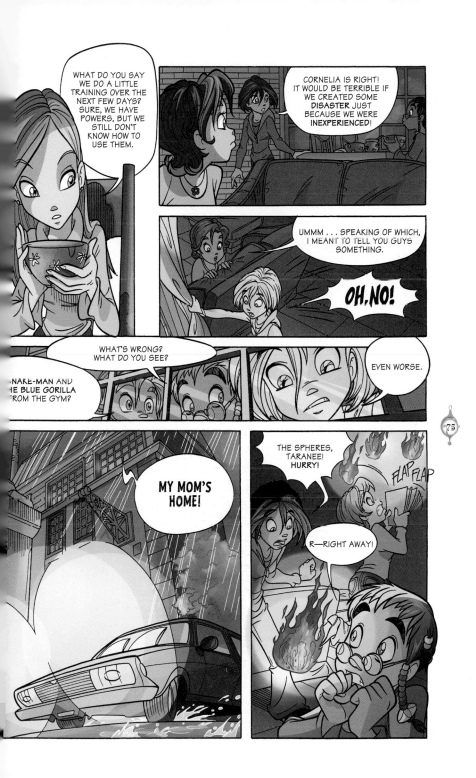

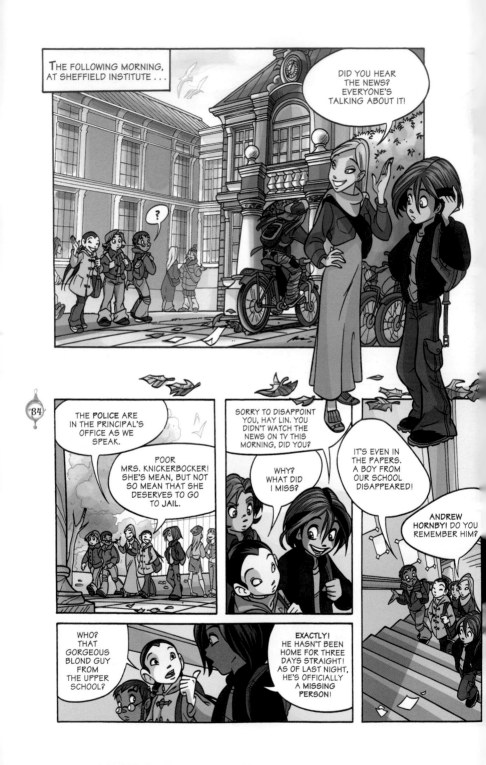

THE SAME WIND THAT BLOWS STRONGLY TODAY, IN THE EATHERFIELD CEMETERY.

T A CHINESE FUNERAL, HITE IS THE COLOR OF OURNING. THE FLOWERS AND PAPER RIBBONS GIVE THE ILLUSION OF NOW, OUT OF SEASON.

IT IS NOT SNOWING, BUT IT IS COLD, JUST THE SAME.

87

GO AHEAD.

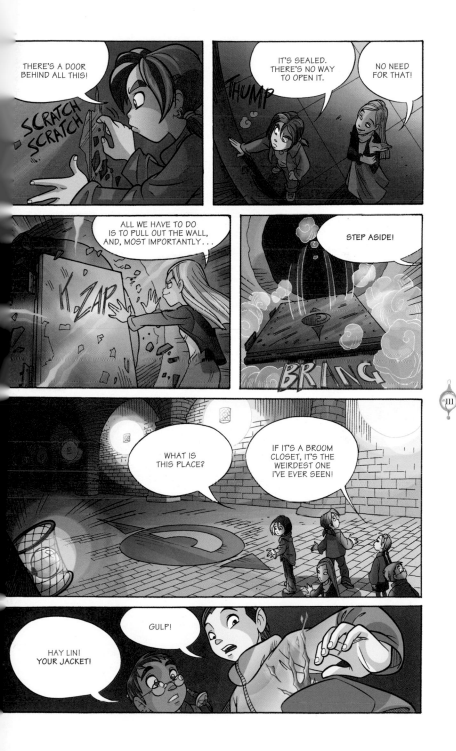